The Hide

and the
Magic Carpet

THE SECRETS OF DROON

The Hidden Stairs
and the
Magic Carpet

by Tony Abbott
Illustrated by Tim Jessell

SCHOLASTIC INC.
New York Toronto London Auckland Sydney
Mexico City New Delhi Hong Kong Buenos Aires

Book design by Dawn Adelman

ISBN-13: 978-0-590-10839-3
ISBN-10: 0-590-10839-5

44 43 42 41 40 39 38 37 36 35 34 33   7 8 9 10 11 12/0

Printed in the U.S.A.   40
First Scholastic printing, June 1999

For Dolores, Jane, and Lucy

Contents

One

The Small Room

Eric Hinkle ran past his mother on his way through the kitchen. He was heading to the back door.

"Neal and I are going to play soccer in the yard," he said. "Julie's coming, too. Gotta go."

"Stop." His mother blocked the door. "Didn't you forget something, Eric?"

She held out her hand.

She was holding empty garbage bags.

Eric looked at his mother. He looked at the garbage bags. All of a sudden, he remembered.

"Oh, no! I forgot about the basement!"

Knock, knock.

Eric sighed. He pulled the door open. Neal Kroger stepped into the kitchen. Neal lived at the end of Eric's street. He was Eric's best friend.

"Hey, what's up?" Neal asked.

"I have to clean the basement," Eric grumbled.

Mrs. Hinkle gave Eric the garbage bags. "You know your father wants to start remodeling the basement soon. This was supposed to be your special job."

Neal made a face at Eric. "That doesn't sound like much fun."

"According to my dad, it's not supposed to be fun," Eric replied. "It's supposed to be done."

"Give it two hours," Mrs. Hinkle said. She pointed to the clock. It was two o'clock.

"Two whole hours?" Eric headed for the basement door.

"Hey, I'll help," said Neal. "We'll be sort of a team. Maybe we'll find some cool stuff."

Eric smiled. Neal is a true friend, he thought. He'll even help clean up junk. "Okay. Come on."

Eric flicked on the light. The two boys tramped down to the basement.

On the right side of the stairs was the playroom. It had paneling on the walls, bookcases, a toy chest, a big sofa, and even a television.

"This looks pretty clean," Neal said, peeking in. "If my basement was like this, I'd live down here."

Eric liked the playroom, too. It was a great place to hang out on rainy days.

"The playroom isn't the problem," Eric said. "Look over here." He stepped into the other side of the basement. The room on the left side of the stairs. The side his father was going to remodel.

"What a mess!" Neal said, looking around.

On one wall was a tool bench filled with jars of nails, nuts, and bolts. On another wall were cabinets lined with canned food. An old washer and drier sat against a third wall.

And everywhere in between was junk. In piles. In bunches. In cartons. In boxes.

There was even a dusty old chair sitting in the middle of the floor.

"We'd better get started," Eric muttered.

Neal slumped into the old chair. "We? Did I say I would help?"

Eric stared at his friend. "You said we were a team."

"I'll be the coach," Neal said with a smile.

Tap, tap!

A face appeared at the basement window.

"It's Julie," said Eric. He waved. "Come in."

Julie Rubin had been friends with Eric and Neal ever since they got stuck in a tree together in kindergarten. Since then, they'd been in all the same classes. They even went to the same summer camp.

"Hi," Julie said as she raced down the stairs. She held a soccer ball under her arm.

"I thought we were going to play," she said, checking her watch. "It's only two o'clock."

Eric dragged a big toy box out from

under the stairs. "Sorry, I've got to clean all this stuff up."

"And I'm coaching," Neal said. "Ball, please?"

Julie passed the ball to Neal and looked around. "It looks like a big job. I'll help."

"How about a little game first?" Neal said. He stood up and bounced the ball once. Then he swung his foot hard. "Heads up, everybody!"

"Wait!" Eric yelled, ducking behind the box.

Too late. The ball was already in the air. It bounced off the tool bench and smacked Neal right in the face. "Ow! My nose!"

"Serves you right!" said Julie.

The ball bounced off the washing machine and rolled into the shadows by the stairs.

"I'll get it!" Julie jumped after the ball, then stopped. "Hey, what's this?" She

pointed to a door in the wall under the stairs. It was open slightly.

"My house has that, too," Neal said. "There's a cool little closet inside."

Eric remembered seeing that door a million times. But he had never been inside. "It must have swung open when I pulled that box away."

"Well, I think the ball went in there," Julie said. She swung the door open further. "Cool!"

Inside was a small closet. The ceiling was the underside of the basement stairs. It slanted all the way to the floor at the back of the room.

In the center sat the soccer ball.

"This is great," Eric said, peeking over Julie's shoulder. "We can put some of the junk in here."

Julie stepped into the room and reached

for the ball. "It's an awesome secret hide-out."

"Let me see!" Neal said. He jumped over to Eric, accidentally pushing him into the door.

Blam! It slammed shut.

A muffled scream came from inside the room.

"Help!" cried Julie. "I'm falling!"

Two

The Sky Below the Ground

Eric pulled the door open quickly.

Julie was standing in the middle of the tiny room. She was staring at the floor beneath her feet. The ball was nowhere in sight.

"Are you okay?" Eric asked.

Julie pushed her way quickly out of the room. "The ball went down there!"

Eric and Neal looked at the gray cement floor. Then they looked back at Julie.

"There were steps," Julie said. "And I almost fell all the way down!"

"Steps?" said Neal. "Where the floor is?"

Julie nodded. "And the soccer ball went bouncing down them. Then you opened the door, and the steps sort of . . . disappeared."

Eric and Neal entered the little room under the stairs. Then Julie stepped back in. They stood close together.

"Maybe the ball whacked you in the head, Julie," Neal said with a laugh. "You just thought there were stairs."

Eric looked down at the floor. There weren't any steps anywhere. "Julie, I don't think —"

"I'm not making this up," she said. "Wait. The door was closed. And it was dark at first. Maybe then . . ."

"It's pretty dark already," Neal said. "Don't close the door on us —"

Slam! Julie did close the door on them.

Neal grumbled. "Now it's very dark."

Then, suddenly, it wasn't.

The floor began to shimmer beneath them, and a bright light glowed under their feet.

Then — *whoosh!* — a stairway appeared out of nowhere. A set of steps, leading down. Leading away from the basement.

Away from the house.

"Whoa!" Eric said. "It looks like *outside* down there! Is this what you saw?"

Julie nodded. "Told you."

The steps glowed a rainbow of colors.

Julie peered over Eric's shoulder. "Let's go find the ball."

Neal reached for the door. "I don't think so."

"Come on," said Eric. He wasn't sure why, but he felt as if they had to go. He stepped down to the next step. Then to the next, and the next. Already the air was brighter where he was. It was pink. And cool and fresh.

"Neal. Julie. This is incredible," Eric said. "We have to go down."

"I don't think this is such a good idea," Neal said.

Julie laughed. She ran to catch up with Eric. "The air smells so sweet! Hurry up, Neal. We're already ten steps ahead of you."

Just below them was a forest of tall trees. The stairs led all the way down to the treetops.

"Unbelievable!" Eric whispered. "Do you think this is some kind of magic?"

"There's no such thing as magic," Julie said, biting her lip. She always did that when she didn't understand why things were happening. "But this place is beautiful. Strange, too. It's sort of like a theme park."

Eric stopped. What he saw coming out of the pink mist was not from any theme park he'd ever been to. "Uh-oh," he gasped.

"What do you see?" Neal asked.

Eric was frozen on the step, pointing into the mist. "Lizards, I think."

"In the trees?" Julie asked. "That's normal."

"No," Eric said. "Flying lizards. Big ones. With weird-looking red guys riding them . . ."

"That's not so normal," Neal said.

Thwang! A long, flaming arrow whistled past Eric's ear.

"Not so friendly, either! They're attacking us!"

Three

Groggles and Ninns

Thwang! Another arrow flew at them. Suddenly, flying lizards were everywhere. The riders on their backs were getting their bows ready for another shot.

"Run back up to my house!" Eric shouted.

"We can't!" Julie said. "The steps are disappearing. Look!" She pointed. The stairs were fading into the mist. Vanishing into the pink sky.

"Oh, man!" Neal cried. "I knew this would happen!"

Thwang! A third flaming arrow shot by.

"Follow me to the bottom," Eric yelled. "We can hide in the trees!" He rushed down, jumping two steps with every jump.

But the steps were disappearing under him.

"No!" he cried. He tumbled into the air.

"Ahhh!" Julie screamed.

Neal shouted, "Grab onto the —"

Eric didn't hear the rest. He fell like a rock through the trees. Branches snapped and cracked around him.

"Umph!" Eric moaned when he finally hit the ground. He lay there, facing the sky. For a second he couldn't remember where he was.

Then he saw the giant lizards circling lower.

Kaww! Kaww! They dived toward him.

"Holy cow!" Eric tried to crawl under a bush.

"Ouch! My ankle!" he groaned. He must have hurt it in the fall. He could hardly move.

The lizards swept even closer to the treetops. When they swooped, Eric saw the riders clearly. Their skin was as bright and shiny as red crayons!

"Oh, man, I must be dreaming!" he whispered to himself. "A really bad dream, too."

"It's bad," said a voice. "But it's no dream."

Eric turned his head. "Who said that?"

"Shhh!" Suddenly the bushes before him began to move, and someone leaped out at him.

It was a girl! She was dressed in a blue

tunic. A thick brown belt was wound around her waist.

Kaww! Kaww! The lizards swooped again.

The girl picked up a pebble. She threw it hard. It hit a distant tree with a loud *smack*.

"Over there!" cried a lizard rider, pointing to the tree. The lizards flew away.

"Whoa, cool move!" Eric looked into the girl's green eyes. Her skin was as pale as a cloud. "But . . . who are you?"

"Keeah," she said. "You must be from the Upper World. How did you get here?"

Eric blinked when he thought of how to tell her. "I . . . uh . . . sort of . . . fell."

"You picked the worst place in all of Droon. Lord Sparr is very close. His red Ninns are everywhere, hunting for me on their flying groggles."

"Lord Sparr?" Eric repeated. "Ninns? Groggles?"

"Did you hurt yourself?" The girl pressed her finger on Eric's ankle.

"Ouch!" Eric grunted.

"It's probably sprained." Then the girl opened a small leather pouch on her wrist. She sprinkled some sparkly dust on Eric's ankle. "Better?"

His leg began to tingle. He moved his foot.

"The pain's gone. How did you do that?"

"Never mind," the girl said. She began to scribble on a piece of paper. "You have to help me. Find Galen and tell him to send this message to my father, King Zello."

"King?" Eric repeated. "You're a princess?"

"There they are! Get them!" a voice cried out from above.

Fwap! Fwap! The lizards dived suddenly toward Keeah and Eric. They flapped to the ground and their red riders leaped off.

"The Ninns have spotted us!" Keeah cried. She pushed the wrinkled scrap of paper into Eric's hand. "Lord Sparr is a wizard. He's pure evil. He will stop at nothing to conquer Droon. Now, hurry. You'll find Galen in his tower."

"Tower?" said Eric. "I can't find any tower. I've got to find my friends and get home!"

The girl looked into his eyes. "If you're from the Upper World, you'll need help getting home. If you do this for me, I promise to help you. Now, I'll distract them while you go. Hurry!"

Without another word, Keeah leaped away swiftly, like a cat. The leaves fluttered above her, and Eric looked up. A strange white bird was gliding over the trees.

The bird seemed to be following her.

"There!" one Ninn yelled. "The princess!"

The red creatures broke branches and tore at leaves to get to Keeah. But she only ran faster.

"I don't believe any of this!" Eric said. He scrambled up from the ground and dashed down a narrow path after the princess. A stone bridge lay ahead of him. Maybe if he got there before the Ninns he could somehow help Keeah escape.

He had to try.

Eric raced toward the bridge.

"Get him!" cried a voice.

A hand came from nowhere.

It grabbed Eric.

It pulled him to the ground!

Four

At the Bridge

"Umph!" Eric rolled over and over until he stopped under the bridge. He looked up.

He couldn't believe his eyes.

"Neal! Julie! I thought I'd lost you — mmmf!"

Neal put his hand over Eric's mouth.

"Shhh!" Julie pointed to the top of the bridge. "Those ugly red guys are up there."

Eric nodded. Neal pulled his hand away.

Eric started speaking as quickly and as softly as he could. He told Neal and Julie what had happened to him.

"We're in someplace called Droon," he whispered. "I met a princess named Keeah. She gave me a message for her father, King Zello."

Neal glanced at the paper in Eric's hand, then gave him a strange look. "Uh-huh. Sure."

"The red guys are called Ninns," Eric continued. "We have to see what they're up to. Give me a boost!"

Neal grumbled but put out his hands so Eric could hoist himself up. A moment later, Julie was next to Eric. Together they peeked over the top of the bridge.

"Uh-oh," Julie whispered.

On the bridge were at least a dozen Ninns.

Up close, their red faces were puffy and

fat. Their slitty eyes were set close to-gether. Their chins were pointed. So were their ears.

On each hand were six clawed fingers.

"Lord Sparr will be angry!" one Ninn snarled.

"The girl's too quick!" snapped another. "And my groggle's too slow." He nodded at his lizard.

Ooga! Ooga! A sound like a horn blasted through the forest. Then the ground rum-bled.

"Is that a car?" Neal whispered from below.

"Uh . . . sort of," Julie answered.

But it wasn't like any car they had ever seen. It was long and yellow and had a bubble on top.

It bounced down the road on eight fat tires.

When it screeched to a stop in front of

the Ninns, a tall man stepped out. He was different from the others, Eric thought. He wasn't a Ninn.

His skin wasn't red, or pale like Keeah's.

He was human . . . pretty much. Well, except for two purple fins sticking up behind his ears.

"Where is the girl?" he snarled. His long black coat dragged heavily across the ground.

The Ninns trembled. One looked up. "The others helped her escape, Lord Sparr," he said.

Lord Sparr's eyes flashed in anger. And the fins behind his ears suddenly grew darker.

"Did you see that?" Julie whispered.

"He's some kind of wizard," Eric whispered back. "Princess Keeah said he was pure evil."

"How many others?" Sparr demanded.

Another Ninn held up his claw. He lowered three of his six fingers. "Three, my lord."

"Scour the forest! Burn it down if you must, but find the girl! Find her friends, too!" Lord Sparr turned and stormed back to his yellow car.

Ooga! Ooga! the horn blasted. The engine roared. The car tore away loudly down the road, leaving a cloud of thick blue smoke behind it.

Fwap! Fwap! The sound of flapping groggle wings filled the forest. A moment later, Eric and his friends were alone at the bridge.

"Lord Sparr is definitely bad news," Julie said. "And those ear fins are very weird."

"This whole place is weird, if you ask

me," Neal said. "How do we get out of here?"

Eric frowned. "Keeah said to find somebody named Galen who lives in a tower. If we do, she promised to help us get home. And Galen is also supposed to send this message to her father."

Eric unfolded the wrinkled paper Keeah had given him. In thin blue ink, it read,

Thginot Dekcatta Eb Lliw Frodnefroz

Eric scratched his head. "Well, this doesn't make any sense."

Julie laughed. "No kidding! I mean, flying lizards, bubble cars, a guy with fins on his head?"

"And all under your stairs," Neal added.

Eric didn't answer. He looked into the forest where he had last seen Keeah. He hoped she was safe. But something told him she wasn't.

"I think she's in danger," he said quietly.

"So are we," Julie added.

"Let's find this Galen guy," Neal said. "The sooner we do, the sooner we get home. There's a path this way. Come on."

Neal started running along the path.

He rushed into a clearing.

And he bumped his nose on something that wasn't there.

Five

The Vanishing Tower

"Oww!" Neal whined, cupping his hands over his face. Then he stared at the empty space in front of him. "Wait. I bumped into . . . nothing?"

Eric stood next to Neal and put his hands out. "No, there's something here. Something hard."

"Hard?" Neal grumbled. "Tell me about it."

"It's over here, too," Julie said as she walked to the other side of the clearing.

Eric went around the other way. "It's round. It must be some kind of — whoa!"

As the three of them stood there, a giant tower shimmered into view. A wooden tower. In fact, it was a tree. But when they touched it, the bark was as hard as stone.

"Hmm," Julie said, biting her lip. "This tree has petrified. It turned to stone because it's so old. We learned about petrified trees at camp."

"I don't remember that," said Neal.

"You were too busy eating snacks," Julie said.

"All that hiking made me hungry," Neal said.

"Guys!" Eric interrupted. "Can you please —"

"Who dares approach the tower of

Galen Longbeard!" cried a voice above them.

They all looked up and gasped.

Crawling slowly down the side of the tower was a large spider with eight long arms and legs. Only it wasn't an ordinary spider. It had a big, round face with large eyes and a pug nose.

And bright orange hair.

Neal nudged Julie. "I sure don't remember anything like *him* at camp," he whispered.

"You aren't Ninns!" the creature squeaked.

"Uh, that's true," Julie said. "Very true."

"In fact, the Ninns are after us," Eric said. "And we have a message from Princess Keeah."

"From the princess?" said the spider. "Then come inside quickly!"

Ploink! A door-sized section of the stony bark swung open.

"I'm Max, a spider troll," he said, jumping into the tree ahead of them. "We must go to the top!"

The three friends piled into the tree.

Together, they crawled up a winding passage and into a large, round room.

The room was cluttered beyond belief.

"Looks like your basement, Eric," Neal said.

Old leather books were stacked up everywhere. Hundreds of tiny colored bottles were collecting dust on deep wooden shelves. A big, ancient mirror leaned against one wall.

And in the center of everything stood a man.

He was tall and thin and very old. He wore a long blue robe and a high cone-shaped hat. His white beard hung down to his belt.

"Behold!" cried Max. "Galen Long-beard, first wizard of Droon! He's more than five hundred years old."

The old man coughed. "Yes, well, welcome to my tower," he said. Then he stroked his beard. "By the way, did anyone see Leep on the way up? Leep is my pilka."

"Uh, what's a pilka, sir?" Julie asked.

Galen cleared his throat. "Well, it's a . . . it has a . . . it goes like . . ." He waved his arms about, trying to describe the lost thing. "Oh, never mind. Leep will turn up somewhere. Now, what brings three Upper Worlders to my tower?"

Eric told Galen what had happened in the forest.

"Here is Keeah's message." Eric handed

the paper to Galen. "It doesn't make sense to us."

The wizard frowned. "Nor to me. Hmm . . ."

"I was thinking," Julie said, looking at the message again. "Maybe it's code. So if the Ninns captured us, they wouldn't understand it."

Galen laughed. "Princess Keeah knows that the Ninns are quite simple. Brains like walnuts. You might even say they are backward."

"Backward?" Neal said. "That's it! I bet Keeah's message is written backward. My sister tries that all the time. But she can't trick me!"

Neal scribbled out the message again, reversing the order of the letters from front to back.

"So . . ." he said. "'Thginot Dekcatta Eb Lliw Frodnefroz' becomes 'Zorfendorf

Will Be Attacked Tonight.' Does that make sense?"

Galen's eyes flashed suddenly. "Zorfendorf Castle! Lord Sparr plans to attack it tonight. I must warn King Zello immediately!"

Before another word was spoken, a blue mist rose around the wizard. Sparks of light streaked through it. Then he mumbled strange sounds.

"Kolo . . . bembo . . . zoot!"

An instant later — *zamm!* He wasn't there!

"Whoa!" Eric gasped. "Where did he —"

But — *zamm!* — Galen was already back. "I've just been to Jaffa City," he said. "King Zello is sending his army to defend Zorfendorf Castle."

"Mission accomplished!" Max chirped. "Sparr is stopped — for the moment."

Galen turned to the children. He looked

grim. "You have entered a troubled world, my young friends. Tell me, how did you come to be here?"

Julie told him how she found the steps in the little room in Eric's basement.

Galen sighed deeply. "Ah, the enchanted staircase. I wondered when it would appear again."

Eric blinked. "So you know about the stairs?"

The wizard walked slowly to a globe of Droon standing against the wall. Half of the globe was dark, half light. He stared at it for a long time.

"Ages ago, Lord Sparr created the Three Powers," Galen said finally. "Objects of unimaginable might. Fearing he would use them to take over your world, I sealed the stairs that once joined our two realms."

"I didn't know we lived in a realm!" said Neal.

"Indeed you do," Galen said. "But now I am old. My ancient spells grow weak. That is why the stairs are visible once again."

"They faded after we came down," Julie said.

Max chittered excitedly. "Keeah can help you find them. She has powers!"

Eric remembered how the princess cured his sprained ankle. "Is Keeah a wizard, too?"

Before Galen could answer, a buzzing sound came from across the room. *Zzzzt!*

Everyone turned to the old mirror. The rippled surface was flickering with a strange glow.

"A big-screen TV!" Neal joked. "How many channels do you get on this thing?"

"I use it to keep watch over Droon," Galen said. He waved his hand, and a scene moved hazily across the surface of the glass. "Like me, this mirror is old. But with it I can see most of what happens." The wizard's eyes widened suddenly in fear. "Oh, dear!"

"What's the matter?" Julie asked.

Galen pointed at the scene coming onto the mirror. It showed a vast black castle.

"Plud!" he gasped.

"Lord Sparr's evil fortress!" Max chittered.

The mirror zoomed in on the fortress.

In the courtyard were two red Ninns. Between them was a girl, struggling to get free.

"It's Keeah!" Eric cried. "The Ninns must have captured her in the woods."

And now she was a prisoner of Lord Sparr!

Six

Home Must Wait

"The forbidden city of Plud," Max said. "The Ninns have taken Princess Keeah to Plud!"

Eric stared at the mirror. "She seems really afraid. What are we going to do?"

"We must go to her!" Galen said, pulling a large sword down from the wall. "Plud is an evil place. It is where Keeah's mother, Queen Relna, fought her last battle against Sparr."

Neal shivered. "You mean, she's dead?"

"She was never seen again," Galen said as he slid the sword into his belt. "But that is not the worst of it. Sparr now seeks from Keeah the Red Eye of Dawn. It is one of the Three Powers I told you about. It is a jewel that commands the forces of nature."

"Does Keeah have it?" Julie asked.

Galen grabbed a helmet from a shelf. "I do not know. Even Keeah doesn't know. To stop Sparr from using the Powers for evil, I cast them to the winds and charmed them to change their shapes. No one knows what they have become."

"But Sparr will stop at nothing to have them again!" Max chittered, scurrying toward the passage to the ground. "I fear for Keeah. Hurry!"

Zzzzt!

"Wait," Julie said, turning back. "The mirror."

The hazy glass showed a city of bright

towers as light and sunny as Plud was dark. In the distance, a black cloud of groggles was descending.

"Sparr has tricked us!" Galen boomed. "His Ninns are attacking Jaffa City! Oh, I hope the princess can defend herself against Sparr until I return. I must go to Jaffa this instant."

"Wait," said Eric, turning to his friends. "Keeah helped me in the forest. And she was going to get us home. Now she's in trouble. I mean, we *have* to help her."

"How can we get to Plud?" Julie asked Galen.

"Hey!" Neal yelled suddenly. He jerked back, tumbling over a stack of books and hitting the floor with a thud. "Something just licked me!"

"Leep?" cried Max. He sprang up and landed in midair. "The pilka! I'm sitting on her!"

Galen quickly pulled at the air under Max. As he did, a silken fabric seemed to collect in his hands. And a creature took shape in the room.

It was an animal the size of a horse. But with long white fur. And six legs. And a friendly face.

It looked like a shaggy camel.

"Pilkas are quite friendly," said Max. "And quite fast! Leep seems to like you, Master Neal."

Hrrrr! The creature whinnied loudly. She plodded to the passage door and turned her head back, as if beckoning the children to follow.

Eric looked around at his friends.

"We're running out of time," Julie said.

Neal nodded. "Plus, we're a team, right?"

Eric felt his heart begin to race. "I guess we're going to Plud!"

Seven

The Forbidden City

"Take Leep at once," Galen told Eric and his friends as they stood outside the tower. "And take this invisible cloak. It may come in handy."

"And take me!" Max twittered. "I may come in handy, too. Besides, I know the way to Plud."

Galen smiled. "Good luck, my young friends, and remember what I am about to tell you. Droon is a secret to your world.

When you return home, tell no one about us. Also, you must not take anything from Droon with you, nor leave anything from the Upper World behind."

"Why?" Eric asked.

"For every object left here, a thing from Droon will appear in your world," the wizard replied.

"And it may not be a good thing!" Max added.

Neal blinked. "You mean like . . . a Ninn?"

"Or worse," Galen said. "Now I must go to Jaffa City and you to Plud. Be careful!"

Then, without another word — *zamm!* — Galen Longbeard, first wizard of Droon, vanished.

And his tower vanished with him.

Hrrr! The shaggy pilka whinnied.

"Well, what are we waiting for?" said Eric.

With the three children on her back and Max sitting on her head, Leep galloped out of the forest. She rode across open meadows while the pink sky darkened into late afternoon. It grew colder as the light faded.

A shape moved across the sky above them.

"Groggles?" said Julie.

Neal looked up. "No," he said. "A falcon. A white one. I think I saw it before, too. I remember falcons from our zoo trip last year."

Eric watched the bird soar away. "This one was in the forest when we first saw Sparr."

Hrrr! Leep whinnied sharply and slowed her gallop.

"Hush now," Max whispered. "We are close."

He pulled the reins, and the pilka plodded up a low hill to a jagged ridge.

The high black walls of a large city loomed before them. The sky was thick with clouds. The air smelled of smoke.

"Let me guess," Neal said. "This is Plud."

The three riders slid to the ground in a grove of trees. Max jumped down with Leep's cloak. "Don't forget this. Invisibility might be useful."

"So would a magic key," Julie said. "Those walls are super high. How do we get in?"

Rrrr! The ground began to rumble.

"A car?" Eric whispered. "Yes, Sparr's car! The gates will open for him. He's our way in!"

Ooga! Sparr's car roared loudly up the road.

Hrrr! The pilka reared, spooking at the sound.

"Leep, wait!" Max shouted. But the animal broke away from him. He scurried down the hill after her. "Leep! Leep!"

"Come back, Max," Julie said. "We need you!"

The car roared by. The gates of Plud opened.

"We're losing our chance," Eric hissed. "Come on!" He grabbed Neal and Julie.

The three of them dashed in after the yellow car. They jumped behind a low wall just as — *chong!* — the huge black gates closed.

Sparr's car screeched to a stop in a courtyard. A group of Ninns raced out to greet their master.

"The princess is in the main tower," one said.

Without a word, Sparr stomped into the fortress. The Ninn guards marched in after him.

"Okay," Eric whispered. "Let's go. Quietly."

They slipped into the fortress. The hallways were as narrow and dark as the streets outside. Ninn footsteps echoed loudly on the stone floors.

Julie stopped. "Wait. Do we have a plan?"

Eric peered into the dark. "There are some steps ahead. If we sneak up to the main tower, maybe we can get to Keeah before Sparr does."

Neal nodded. "And get back out, too. Right?"

"Of course," Eric said.

"Sounds good," said Julie. "Lead on."

They tiptoed up the long stairway. After what seemed like hundreds of steps they reached the top of the main tower. At the end of a short hallway was a door. Two big Ninns in black armor guarded it.

"Do we have to . . . fight them?" Neal whispered, out of breath.

Eric shook his head. "No. Now we use some magic." He pulled Galen's cloak over himself.

"I like it," Julie said. "Poof, you're gone!"

"Hide in the shadows," Eric said. Then, completely invisible, he slipped down the hall.

He jabbed one of the guards in the shoulder.

"Stop that!" the Ninn yelled. He swatted the other Ninn in the arm.

"I didn't do anything!" the second Ninn cried. He whacked the other on his shiny black helmet.

"I'll get you for that!" the first Ninn yelled.

"Not if I get you first!" the other growled, butting the first one on the head and chasing him right past the kids and down the stairs!

A moment later, the hallway was clear.

"Great job!" Julie said as Eric pulled off the cloak and looped it around his belt.

"I'll stand guard outside," Neal said. "You two go in and get the princess."

Eric and Julie unbolted the door and pushed it open. They entered a small, dark room.

Princess Keeah was sitting on the floor. She looked up and jumped. "The boy in the woods!"

Eric grinned. "We've come to rescue you!"

Keeah smiled. "I knew someone would come." Then her smile faded. "But if we're going to get out of here at all, we need to hurry!"

As quickly as she had run through the forest, Keeah scampered from the room and down the hallway. Eric, Julie, and Neal followed her.

"Sparr thinks I have the Red Eye of Dawn," Keeah whispered. "With it, he plans to conquer all of Droon!"

"And so I shall, Princess Keeah!"

The four children froze in the dark hall.

Out of the shadows stepped Lord Sparr.

Eight

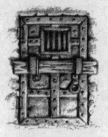

Prisoners!

Clomp! Clomp! The children were marched to a room at the top of another tower. A dozen Ninn warriors in shiny black armor surrounded them.

Clang! The iron door was bolted shut.

They were prisoners.

Lord Sparr paced back and forth before a thick blue curtain that covered one of the walls.

"Princess Keeah," he began. "You and

your friends spoiled my plans to attack Zorfendorf Castle. And Galen discovered my little raid on Jaffa City. No matter. Having *you* as a prisoner is far more valuable. Besides, you have something that belongs to me."

The princess backed away. "Let us go, Sparr. My father is on his way here right now."

Sparr laughed. "Neither your father nor your mother will ever see you again."

"My mother died," Keeah said. "And my —"

The sorcerer smirked. "Your mother is —" Then he stopped. His eyes flashed. "That leather pouch on your wrist . . ."

"What?" Keeah said.

Sparr grabbed the pouch from Keeah.

"My mother gave me that!" she cried, trying to take it back.

But Sparr held it high. His fins turned

inky black. He began to shake. "O jewel, if it be you, show me now your shape so true!"

At once, the pouch began to shrink in Sparr's palm. It shriveled to the size of a small egg.

Then it turned very smooth.

Then it turned red.

It began to glow.

"No . . ." Keeah gasped. "No . . . no!"

Sparr howled. "The Red Eye of Dawn! You had it all along! Now I have it. The First Power is mine once again!"

"Give it back to her, you smelly fish head!" Eric yelled. He rushed at Sparr, but one of the Ninns grabbed him and pushed him roughly into Julie and Neal. Then the sorcerer spoke words that made their blood turn to ice.

"I . . . know . . . you . . . three. . . ."

"What?" Julie said. "How could you —"

"You are from the Upper World. You

have found the stairs. *My* stairs." Sparr pointed at Eric. "They are . . . in your house!"

Eric shuddered. "How do you know that?"

"I know many things about you," Sparr said. Then he reached back and tore the blue curtain aside.

"Uh-oh," Neal whispered.

Behind the curtain was a tall display stand. On the stand was a round black-and-white object.

"Our soccer ball!" Julie exclaimed.

"I have learned much from this object," Sparr said, hovering over the ball. "But not as much as I shall learn . . . when I am done with you."

Suddenly, a voice cried shrilly from the window. "You are done right now, Sparr!"

Everyone turned to see a mop of orange hair scurry down the wall.

"Max!" Julie cried.

"The one and only!" Max jumped to the floor and quickly spun a sticky web of threads around the Ninns' feet. "Ha-ha!" he chittered.

"G-g-g-guards!" Lord Sparr sputtered. "Take them all to the dungeon!"

His red warriors lunged at the children.

And tripped on Max's gooey web!

"All right!" Eric cried, leaping for the soccer ball and tossing it high. "Neal! Your famous bad kick! Just like in my basement!"

Neal grinned. "Heads up, everybody!" He jumped at the ball and kicked it hard.

"Akkk!" One Ninn groaned. "My nose!"

"Serves you right!" Julie shouted. She snuck up and kicked the ball again. This time, it went straight for another Ninn's stomach. He fell back into two others, knocking them to the floor.

"Score!" Eric said, diving for the ball.

"I'll get the Red Eye of Dawn!" Keeah cried.

But Sparr spun around and raised his fist.

Kla-blam! A bolt of red fire shot from his hand. He staggered backward as the fire blew past Keeah, punching a hole straight through the wall to the hall outside.

"We'll get the Eye later!" Eric shouted. "Everybody out!" He jumped through the hole in the wall with Neal and Keeah. Julie and Max ran after them. They all rushed down the hall.

But the Ninns were right on their heels.

"This way!" said Eric, tumbling through a narrow door. He tossed the soccer ball to Julie and slammed the door behind them.

"Uh-oh," said Neal as he looked around.

Dim light from a high window showed that they were in a small room.

A very small room.

"Uh-oh is right," Julie said. "I think we found a dungeon all by ourselves!"

Nine

Into Thin Air!

Wham! Wham! The Ninns battered the door, but Eric and Neal held it as tight as they could.

"Dungeons don't have exits," Max said, crawling to the window. "This is a storage room."

"Too bad it's not a *magic* storage room," Julie said. "The invisible cloak isn't big enough for all of us. And there's nothing here but these dumb old rugs."

"Rugs?" said Keeah. "They might be old, but . . . maybe they're not so dumb. Check the label."

Clonk! The Ninns banged harder on the door.

Julie read the label. "It says, 'Rugs by Pasha. Do not remove this tag.'"

Keeah's face lit up. She nearly laughed. "Find a green one with purple spirals in the corners."

"This is no time to pick out a rug!" Eric said.

"Not just any rug," Keeah said. "A Pasha original." She helped Julie tug out one big carpet. They spread it on the floor.

Kkkrrkk! The door started to splinter.

Eric felt his strength slipping away. "We can't hold this door much longer!"

"Everyone on!" Keeah said, sitting on the rug.

Julie jumped on. "Now what? We fly?"

Suddenly, the carpet lifted from the floor.

"Yikes!" Julie gasped. "I guess we do!"

Keeah laughed. "The carpet must like your voice. Pasha's rugs don't fly for just anybody."

Julie shrugged. "All I said was . . . fly."

Swoosh! The carpet circled the room!

Blam! The door shook. One of its hinges blasted off.

Max strained with his thin arms and pried the window open. Cold air swirled in from outside.

"Max! Eric! Neal!" Julie cried. "Get on the rug!"

"No," said Max. "I must go save Leep. Besides, I don't ride rugs. I get airsick, you know!"

Waving with three of his arms, Max scrambled out the window and down to the ground below.

Neal jumped onto the rug, holding the soccer ball between his legs. "Whoa! It's wobbly up here!" He clung to the long fringe and held out a hand to Eric. "Grab on, pal!"

Kkkrunch! The door burst open, and a dozen Ninns rushed in, with Lord Sparr in the lead.

Eric leaped to the carpet.

"I *will* stop you!" Sparr cried. He thrust his fist at them. "Red Eye of Dawn, give me the power!"

Kla-bbblam! Bolts of jagged fire exploded in the room just as the carpet slid out the window.

The rug pulled away into the air. But Sparr aimed his fist again.

"He's going to blast us!" Neal yelled.

Suddenly, the white falcon was there, tearing out of the clouds! It swooped with incredible speed, right at Sparr.

"It's attacking him!" Keeah cried.

Ka-whoom! The flame from the red jewel seemed to engulf Sparr's hand. He stumbled back, his face twisted in pain, as the fiery bolts flew harmlessly into the air.

"Missed by a mile!" yelled Julie. She steered the rug higher and higher into the sky.

"I will hunt you down!" Sparr shouted. But the falcon swooped again, driving him back from the window.

Swoosh! The carpet lifted up from the fortress.

"Yahoo!" Eric yelled as they soared into the sky.

He was still yelling when they disappeared behind the clouds.

Ten

The World Under the Stairs

Swoosh! Swoosh!

Pink air swirled all around the flying carpet.

"We did it! We're free!" cried Keeah. She looked over the side until Plud was a tiny dot on the ground. Then she turned to Eric.

"Thank you. You helped me, even though you didn't know me. Now let me get you home."

Eric scanned the distance. "The magic

stairs faded. I don't know where they are now."

"I saw them in a dream once," Keeah said, narrowing her eyes. "They were in the ice hills of Tarabat. Let's try there. Julie, head north!"

Julie pulled hard, and the rug swept upward.

As they flew, snow began to swirl in the air. Cold winds howled over them. A few minutes later, they were swerving through narrow mountain passes and over icy peaks.

Suddenly, a rainbow of colors glistened ahead of them.

"There it is!" cried Neal. "We found it!"

Julie tugged a fringe. The carpet dipped toward the hills. It slowed and hovered at the foot of the stairs.

The three friends hopped to the bottom step.

Eric turned to Keeah. "Galen was right. We did enter a world in trouble."

Keeah nodded. "But a world with hope, too. Thanks to all of you, I can keep fighting Lord Sparr."

Eric handed her Galen's invisible cloak. "Galen said we can't take anything with us."

Keeah smiled. She held the soccer ball in her hands for a moment, then tossed it to Eric. "And don't leave anything behind!"

Then she tugged on the carpet. Obediently, it pulled away from the steps.

"Will we see you again?" Eric called out.

The icy air began to sing all around Keeah. "If the magic works, you will!"

A moment later, she soared over the hills.

Eric stared into the snowy air until she was gone. "If the magic works?"

"Better hurry," Julie said, starting up the steps, "or we'll be stuck in this snowstorm forever."

The three friends ran up the stairs and entered the small room in Eric's basement.

Eric turned to take one last look at the strange world of snow beneath them.

"Good-bye, Droon," he said. He touched the wall next to him. *Click!* The light went on.

The cement floor instantly took shape beneath them. The world under the stairs disappeared.

As if it had never existed.

The three friends just stared at one another for a long time. Finally Eric opened the door and walked out into the basement. It was still cluttered and messy.

"I don't know," he said, dropping the soccer ball onto the dusty chair. "It does seem kind of impossible, doesn't it?"

"Oh, yeah?" Neal said, holding his stomach. "I still feel that rug bouncing under me."

"And we helped Keeah," Julie said. "That was real. It was too cool *not* to be real!"

Eric slid a box in front of the door. "Galen told us to keep Droon a secret. And Keeah said we'll know we're going back, 'if the magic works.' Until then, I guess we just have to wait."

Julie checked her watch. "We've been gone for hours. We'd better tell our parents we're okay."

Together they tramped up to the kitchen. Eric took a deep breath and opened the door.

His mother was sitting at the dinner table. She had a shocked look on her face. "Eric?"

"Mom, let me try to explain. We —"

"Eric," she said, "you'll never get the job done if you give up so soon." She pointed to the clock.

It was only ten minutes after two.

"We did all that *in ten minutes?*" Neal said.

Julie's mouth dropped open. "That means —"

Mrs. Hinkle stood up. "You've finished the entire basement?" She started for the door.

"Mom, no!" Eric said, blocking the door. "Actually, we didn't get far. There's still a lot to do."

She glared at him. "Because after the basement is the attic. And the porch. And the garage —"

Wham! The basement door slammed shut as Eric and his friends rushed back down the stairs.

They stopped at the bottom and stared.

Floating silently in the middle of the messy room was the soccer ball. Across the surface of the ball were letters written in thin blue ink.

Nruter Ot Uoy Llet Lliw Smaerd Ruoy

"A message from Keeah!" Eric cried.

Neal studied the words. "It says, 'Your dreams will tell you to return.'"

Suddenly, the patches of black and white swirled across the surface of the soccer ball, forming the ragged shapes of countries.

"It's a globe," said Julie. "A globe of Droon!"

The globe floated magically for a few moments, then changed back into a ball again.

It dropped into Eric's hands.

"Whoa!" he gasped. "Guys, I'm no wizard, but I'm pretty sure the magic is working!"

"Me, too," said Neal. "I say we go home tonight and do some serious dreaming!"

Julie nodded. "And we keep on dreaming —"

"— until we get back to Droon!" Eric said.

Then the three friends laughed out loud together.

"To Droon!" they cheered.

ABOUT THE AUTHOR

Tony Abbott is the author of more than two dozen funny novels for young readers, including the popular *Danger Guys* books and *The Weird Zone* series. Since childhood he has been drawn to stories that challenge the imagination, and, like Eric, Julie, and Neal, he often dreamed of finding doors that open to other worlds. Now that he is older — though not quite as old as Galen Longbeard — he believes he may have found some of those doors. They are called books. Tony Abbott was born in Ohio and now lives with his wife and two daughters in Connecticut.

The Adventure Continues . . .

**Journey
to the
Volcano Palace**

Moments later, the sun began to rise over the distant dunes.

"It's time!" Keeah said.

They all climbed to the rim of a tall, curving sand dune. Galen pointed to the sandy plains where the sun was rising.

"The door to Kano lies in the East," the wizard said. "According to a legend, it can be seen where it is not."

Eric nodded slowly. "Okay. Got it. Great. Um . . . could you say that again?"

"It's a riddle," Max said, scurrying back and forth in the sand. "No one knows exactly where Sparr's palace is."

Julie began biting her lip again. "Then how are we going to find the door to Kano?"

But Galen was already walking back down the dune. "By finding the answer to the riddle!"

"First things first," Khan said. "Our journey of many miles begins with a single sniff!" He sniffed the air, then pointed. "East is that way!"

Within moments, Khan and his Lumpies packed up the tent and supplies.

"Into the East!" Max chirped.

Hrrr! Galen's shaggy pilka, Leep, whinnied in excitement as the kids piled onto her back.

"We're off!" cried Julie.

They rode for hours over the hot dunes.

Mile after mile, they saw nothing but burning white sand.

"I think we're lost," Neal said, wiping his forehead. "I mean, I guess we're in the East, but I don't see any doors. All I see are two things. Sand, and more sand."

Eric pointed into the distance. "What's that?"

It looked like a shadow against the far-away dunes, a grove of trees waving in the breeze.

"Is it a mirage?" Julie said. "You know, the imaginary things you see in the desert that aren't really there?"

"Imaginary," Eric sighed. "Right now I'm imagining the town pool filled with cool water."

"You want water, you got it," Neal said. "I'm gonna be a puddle in about three minutes."

"No, you won't," Keeah said. "That's an oasis! We can rest there and get some real water!"

They rode quickly and soon reached a

group of tall palm trees sprouting up from the dunes.

In the center was a pool of cool, blue water.

Eric and his friends slid down from Leep and moved into the shade of the waving palm trees.

"This isn't the pool in my dream," Julie said. "There's nothing yucky about this."

"Good!" Neal exclaimed. "Because I'm *way* past thirsty." He and Julie and Keeah went to the near side of the pool and began to drink.

The Lumpies led the pilkas over. They all bent their heads to the water.

"Drink up," Khan said. "It may be many miles before we are able to find water again."

Eric scrambled to an open spot on the side of the pool. He breathed in the sweet air under the trees, then bent down, cupping his hands together. The shimmering water looked so refreshing.

He stooped to take a big sip.

He froze solid at what he saw.

"What is it?" Keeah said, looking up.

Eric stared into the pool. "My reflection —"

Neal laughed. "Yeah, you look pretty grimy!"

"We all do," Julie added.

"No, that's not it," Eric mumbled. In the surface of the pool he saw his face. Behind his head were the tops of the palm trees that he knew were waving in the wind behind him.

And behind the palm trees . . . was an enormous gate! A gate made of black iron, towering up behind the palms.

Eric whirled around and looked up.

There was no gate behind the palm trees.

He turned back to the pool. The gate was there, in the reflection, standing as huge and as plain as day!

"An invisible gate!" he gasped. "Like the riddle says — it can be seen where it is not!"

THE SECRETS OF DROON

By Tony Abbott

Read them all!

Under the stairs, a magical world awaits you!

SCHOLASTIC

www.scholastic.com/droon

SODBL0507